DERANGED DREAMS

&

STRAITJACKET SCREAMS

C. J. CANNATELLI

{ 2 }

For my dear friend,
Gillian "Orla" Harding

You are, by far, the most committed to my work. I can't stress enough how your actions have honestly helped me find a meaning in life. Thank you, Orla. You are the closest thing to a sister I will ever have.

TABLE OF CONTENTS

BEELZEBUB'S BIG-TIME BAKERY

THE VERMONT INCIDENT

DEVIL'S DELINQUENTS

GREY

GRANDDADDY

TO GIVE UP SMOKING

BEHIND THE SHOWER CURTAIN

BEELZEBUB'S BIG-TIME BAKERY

Aaron Chase's walk home from the bus stop every Monday through Friday at around five in the evening had become an unbearable task for him. With age, his thigh muscles cried out silently in agony. Every day was the same, monotonous routine that dulled his mind to the world around him. Aaron Chase was slowly growing old enough to retire.

As he took his arduous route home, he found himself parallel to the run-down park across the street. To his right was a mile of abandoned buildings. Or at least, he had always believed them to be abandoned. Aaron cursed under his breath as the sky let out a cacophony of thunder so monstrous that he questioned whether or not this was the beginning of the next great flood.

When he reached the end of the block, he was absolutely drenched with rain water. His eyes scanned the surrounding buildings as he pled silently to find shelter from the storm. Any open building would do. Aaron had to do a double-take when he saw he was standing in front of what appeared to be a newly-renovated storefront. The building stood out in comparison to its dilapidated neighboring structures. This place was painted a pastel shade of mint green with a sign scrawled above the double doors written in a bubbly script.

Beelzebub's Big-Time Bakery.

Not giving the name a second thought, Aaron rushed into the building for shelter so quickly that his briefcase fell open; its paper contents spilling out of it like a mudslide. Aaron once again swore angrily under his breath as he bent down in humiliation, rushing to gather his scattered belongings. He hadn't noticed the man leaving his space behind the counter to help him.

"Having a shit day, I see, sir," the man said to Aaron. "If I'm not intruding."

"Sorry to rush in here like this," Aaron said shamefully. "The rain—"

"We all have our bad days, son," the man laughed. "Call me Lucky. All my best pals call me Lucky."

"So, Lucky," Aaron smiled. He glanced around at the delicacies encased in glass. "Do you run this bakery?"

"Sure do," Lucky confirmed with a chuckle. "All you gotta do is tell me what you want most out of life."

Aaron's face contorted into a perplexed expression. No one had ever posed such a question to him in that manner, let alone a complete stranger. Aaron contemplated his response. Judging from the mile-long gaze Lucky wore, he was being serious. A hint of curiosity glistened in his radiant green eyes.

Aaron took a moment to think about his words carefully. Growing up, Aaron's father had always taught him to select his words with caution. Aaron thought briefly about the chaotic, swirling shit-storm that his life had become. He worked a dead-end desk job at a company he didn't give a damn about. His boss hated him. He had no living relatives or friends to speak of. The only time anyone seemed to notice Aaron was when the marshal showed up at his door earlier that day to serve him with an eviction notice.

"I wish I were dead," Aaron said flatly.

Lucky clapped his hands together and belted out a roar of laughter. He scurried behind the counter and selected a cupcake from the case. It had pink frosting on it.

"Then, my good sir, I'd like you to have this," Lucky said, approaching Aaron and shoving the cupcake into his palm. "This one's on the house."

Aaron let out a quiet chuckle. He had never gotten a damned thing for free in his entire life. Now, he was getting a cupcake. It certainly brought a smile to Aaron's face. He quickly devoured the cupcake, knowing that it would probably be a very long time before he had something so sweet again.

"There, there," Lucky said, leading Aaron over to a chair in the corner of the room. "You'll get your wish. I run a business, but hell, can't a man enjoy baking and harvesting the souls of the living *simultaneously*? Geez, society is so high-strung—"

"What?" Aaron gasped. "Souls of the living?"

Aaron's body seemed to lock up. At first, he thought it was fear. Then he remembered his days in college and his experimental drug usage. He had overdosed quite a few times and barely lived to tell the tale. This was a familiar feeling. His entire body stung with the sensation of a thousand pins and needles, jabbing through his flesh and giving Aaron a glimpse at his own mortality.

"Oh, this one's a *piece of cake*," Lucky chuckled. "See, you'll be dead before I finish explaining. That cupcake was a contract. Since you've accepted a favor from me, I am sure you are well aware of the price—"

"You're not the devil," Aaron gasped, trying desperately to regain control of his body. Aaron's bladder gave out, leaving a steady stream of urine sliding down his pant leg.

"I'm a crown King of Hell, thank you kindly," Lucky giggled. "Beelzebub is the name, soul-snatching is the game."

Aaron's world collapsed into a realm of darkness. As his eyes closed for the final time, Beelzebub, a very lucky demon, snapped his fingers once and it were as though Aaron had never even been there. This was, of course, the perfect location to run such an operation. Those who seek nothing will receive nothing. They will walk by an abandoned building without a second thought. Lucky really did love rainy days like this, because the customers seemed so eager to come inside wherever they could; even if they entered the Devil's workshop, just to get away from the violent wind and falling water droplets. Beelzebub stood up and greeted his next customer.

THE VERMONT INCIDENT

I won't give my name here simply because if you have any interest in the paranormal, cryptozoology, or freakishly bizarre and unexplainable occurrences, you would recognize my work. If you believe in this shit, I'm your worst fucking nightmare. I will say that I am a married woman in my early thirties living in New England. My wife is my investigative partner. For the purpose of this story, we will call my wife Dianne. That's all you need to know about me, as I am not the subject of this event.

To clarify, I do not *believe* in cryptids, ghosts or monsters. I have dedicated my life to disproving fraudulent, pseudoscientific information being spread about things that don't exist. Through the years, billions of dollars have been wasted investigating such wild claims. The saddest part, for me, is all the people who have wasted their lives on something they truly believed in. Then again, you could argue that I've wasted my life on something, determined to destroy the frauds you see in the media. I'm a professional debunker, so to speak.

Throughout my years, I have outed many "psychics", cryptozoologists and general con artists. I have destroyed their careers. Ever wonder what happened to ll those ghost hunting shows and why they never last long? They're staged. And can prove it. And I have proven it time and time again. But that's a story for nother day.

I guess you can say this story began (for me, anyway) in mid to late 2003. I was in Mexico for a month, researching a series of cryptid sightings that I won't get into too much detail about. Basically, I spent a month chasing down leads and eventually staked out the locations, only to disprove it by capturing the "creature". It was a rabid dog. Some people will put you through hell if they think they can make a quick cameo on the local news.

I got a call from our office as Dianne was driving us back to the United States, where we would return the rental car, hop on a plane to New England and write a very angry article on the fraudulent news reporting. One of our researchers got his hands on a few police reports filed in upstate New York, both of which were from the same couple.

Now, the public has a tendency to think that "police report" translates into "evidence to be used as fact." He gave me a summary of the reports, but names had been redacted. That piqued my interest, as typically, the names of these people are typically out there in the open because they want attention.

The first report was for a missing child, the couple's son. The family owned a large home with a lot of land and allegedly, the father was watching his son outside when he became distracted with a newspaper. The father noticed this young boy heading into the woods and he called for him to stay in the yard. The father then proceeded to get distracted again for approximately three minutes. At this point, he looked up from his newspaper and his child was gone. The father didn't immediately panic, assuming the little boy couldn't have gone far. He entered the woods at approximately 3:15pm to look for his son. After five or ten minutes, the father began to panic. He decided to run inside to call the police, but on his way back, he saw a yellow piece of fabric on the ground about twenty feet away from where he was walking. He remembered his son had been wearing a yellow shirt and hurried to the object, finding that the shirt had been torn to pieces and was soaked with blood. Police were called and search parties were launched. Within the next three days, they found one of the boy's shoes and his baseball. The boy's body has never been found.

I was skeptical as to where my researcher was going with this. So a kid ran off in the woods and got himself mauled by a bear or something. How did this concern me? The second report was filed six days after the boy's disappearance. The couple also had a daughter, who was two years younger than her brother. She slept in a bedroom across the hall from their bedroom, located on the second floor of the house. The father came into the bedroom, complaining about hearing noises that appeared to be coming from the attic. The couple assumed it was an animal and went to bed. A few hours later, at approximately 2:35am, the couple awoke to a loud crash coming from somewhere in the house. The parents were immediately on their feet, rushing to check on their daughter, who was now screaming. The parents entered the bedroom and saw a crouched, hairless figure with gray skin and sunken black eyes. It was hovering over their daughter's bed. The creature caught sight of them and crawled out of the now broken second-story bedroom window. The mother rushed to her daughter, who was dead while the father was on the phone with the operator. Her body was completely mangled, but my researcher spared me the details.

At first, I laughed at him. I know it sounds harsh, but I was *not* about to get involved in two parents guilty of killing both of their kids and blaming some monster in the woods. My researcher insisted that he only brought it up because sightings of this creature had been reported all throughout New England. I asked for a more in-depth description of what we were looking for and my researcher paused for a long moment.

"Here's the thing," he said, coughing quietly before continuing. "This isn't exactly recent. Yes, there have been an uptick in accounts in New England, but this definitely mirrors a lot of classical folklore. The people up in New England are calling this thing the Rake for some reason I'm unsure of."

I muffled a laugh. "The *Rake*? Is this a joke?"

"We can't find a source on where the name came from," he sighed. "But similar accounts have been reported by the Navajo reservations on the other side of the country, but they call them—"

"Skin-walkers," I sighed, cutting him off. "God, will they give it up already? It's been debunked for several reasons. The primary reason is that it is described as being a witch using animalistic forms, but if it were in the shape of an animal, all the vocal chords wouldn't be able to—"

"Emulate voices, I know," he said. "But the physical description is there regardless. Then again, leave Navajo legends out of this. I've seen some people claim a stray dog was really a Skin-walker. None of those accounts are credible, as it's the whole 'my uncle's cousin's sister's neighbor' bull shit. Urban legend."

"At least be respectful about it," I joked. "These people actually believe this. I'm in the business of debunking *frauds*, not religions."

"I know, I know," he said. "You and Dianne are scheduled for a cabin in Vermont tomorrow afternoon. You'll be there from tomorrow until next week Sunday. Ten days should be fine. It's in the middle of fucking nowhere, and every single resident of this bullshit excuse for a town has supposedly seen the Rake. They've basically closed off half the town because they're terrified. You'll be in the epicenter, where the first sightings occurred. The family has evacuated and you have a lot of ground to cover. It's a big property."

I sighed, explained to Dianne that we wouldn't be home for almost another two weeks and had to wait at the airport for three hours to get on a flight to Vermont instead of our original destination. Then there was the issue of spending hundreds of dollars to check all of the baggage with cameras and equipment. We never travel light.

Fast forward to us arriving on the side of a small town in Vermont that had been virtually quarantined by a local, small-town police chief with nothing better to do with his time. I showed him my credentials, he promised to pray for us and I rolled my eyes.

The cabin was large, but it was by no means luxurious. I let Dianne stay in the house and unpack everything while I spent two hours setting up our equipment as far into the surrounding woods as I was willing to go. Waste of time, now that I think about it. Waste of fucking time.

That night, I let Dianne sleep as she had been driving like crazy for the past month. I sat in front of our command station and, with the help of a case of energy drinks, watched the monitors all night. We had sixty-two cameras I had to constantly be checking. At around one in the morning, I finally found something. All in the span of about ten minutes, forty-seven of our cameras had been "inactive." This means the cameras were not recording and had most likely been severely damaged, likely beyond repair. In all my years, nothing like this has ever happened before. Sure, I've lost a few devices here or there and occasionally a couple would go offline temporarily, but these cameras had clearly been tampered with. I was fucking livid. I firmly believed that some local hicks were fucking with my equipment to try and scare me off. I was having none of that.

    I put on some warm clothes, was quiet as to not wake Dianne and realized I had no choice but to go see what the fuck was going on. I didn't believe in God at the time, but I know a higher power was looking out for me that night. Not only did I remember the combination to our gun safe, but I had the sense not to bring Dianne with me. My greatest fear is losing Dianne and as she is asthmatic, she would not have been able to run. She would have died that night, like I almost did.

    I don't know why, but I kept the gun loaded. I was originally planning to use it to scare off whatever rednecks were fucking with over $250,000 in equipment. Something in my gut told me to load it, check it twice and put extra rounds in the pocket of my trench coat. I carried a small, but very bright flashlight and began my journey into the surrounding woods. I immediately headed in the direction of the damaged cameras.

It took me about twenty minutes to finally reach the location of the damaged cameras. Along the way, all of the cameras I checked were functioning. I jogged most of the way, only stopping to examine equipment. I didn't feel good about leaving Dianne alone in the house with a bunch of crazed hillbillies running around.

When I reached the first set of damaged audio and video equipment, I instinctually cocked my gun. No rednecks could have done this amount of damage. These cameras were *mauled* and half of them appeared to be *bitten*. I realize now that it may have been because they definitely appeared to be out of place. They were red in comparison to the green and brown surroundings. This would likely make them a target to any *real* predators. For the first time in my life, I began to believe in something without seeing it first-hand. With a shaky hand, I reached in my pocket and pulled out my audio recorder that I used for memos. If I was going to die in these woods, I would leave Dianne one final message. I whispered into the recorder, letting her know why I was out there, what I initially was thinking, what I saw, and that I loved her more than anything in this world. Tears filled my eyes as I turned off the recorder, realizing that if the stories were true, Dianne would never get to hear my last words. The recorder would likely be lost, gone the same way my body would be.

Holding my gun at the ready, I began backtracking. I tried to stay as silent as possible. The realization that no human could do such damage to my equipment left me praying that I would make it back to the cabin. I was gonna fucking take Dianne and we would hide in the crawlspace until morning.

I stopped walking when I heard a very strange sound coming from somewhere to my left. It wasn't consistent with human footsteps. It sounded more *erratic*; less controlled. Whatever it was, it sounded like it was walking on more than two limbs. And it was moving fast.

In a flash, I turned to face the noise, standing my ground as my training had taught me. I had the upper hand. I had a loaded firearm and this animal, this *creature* couldn't hurt me. At least, that's what I kept trying to tell myself. With quivering hands, I stared into the trees, catching a glimpse of something gray. My researcher's words replayed in my mind, but I didn't want to get trigger happy and kill some hick having a laugh.

"Show yourself!" I screamed, standing my ground and masking my terror. "I've got a gun!"

This was when it happened. All at once, this creature…the *Rake*, emerged from the bushes and trees. It moved so unnaturally, limbs flailing and looking like something out of that movie, *The Grudge*. It just didn't move like any animal I'd ever seen before. It was hunched over and about three feet tall in that position, leading me to believe that if it could stand up straight, it would tower over me at around six or seven feet. I'm a tall girl, but I had nothing on this thing. I think my aggressive yelling caught it off guard and I think the flashlight confused it. It let out a high-pitched cry and for a brief moment, I thought it feared me. I was dead wrong. It wasn't a wail of fear. It was a battle cry.

In two seconds, the thing was about two feet away from me. I unloaded my entire clip, shooting at it wildly and missing most of my shots. One shot, however, appeared to hit it in the arm or the shoulder, I couldn't be sure. Wherever I hit it, it slowed it down substantially. I didn't waste time. I turned around and hauled ass, reloading my gun as my combat boots sunk into the mud beneath my feet. After I made it a few yards, I heard it running after me, but slower this time. I turned around for a brief moment, emptying my second clip on the thing. This time, it ran behind a tree.

Once again, I ran and reloaded. I didn't hear it following me, but I didn't slow down. Before I knew it, I burst through the back door of the house and locked it. I ran into the hallway and began pushing a massive bookcase in front of the door. I made so much noise, Dianne came running down the stairs. I didn't have time to explain, so I reached in my pocket, handed her my recorder and told her to listen to the last ten minutes. I had to physically grab my wife by the arm as I pulled down the staircase from the ceiling. I shoved her up the stairs, refusing to hear any of her demands for answers. All I kept repeating was four simple words.

"Listen to the tape."

Once I was sure Dianne was secure in the crawlspace, I grabbed both sides of her face and kissed her for a long moment. I had to defend her, even if it meant losing my life to do so. She had already heard most of what happened from the recording and sobbed loudly, begging me to hide with her. I told her I would protect her and closed the staircase, trapping her inside.

I darted to the control station and realized my server was completely down. That meant, in short, that I could see the six remaining cameras surrounding the house, but they would not record. I heard Dianne sobbing quietly, but I knew that was because I was in the room right below her crawlspace. I searched desperately to find the heavy-duty guns we kept for emergencies like these. It took me several attempts to get the combination on the locks right because of how shaky my hands were. I watched the cameras, loading my rifle and lighting a cigarette. I grabbed a half empty bottle of scotch from the dresser and took a long swig. I nearly spit it out when I saw the creature crawling on one of the cameras. Then another. It was circling the house, but it seemed injured. Twenty minutes before the sun came up, the creature was gone and I had packed everything we had, keeping a close eye on the cameras. Armed to the teeth, I brought everything to the car. I didn't want Dianne to panic. The moment the sun illuminated the world, I got Dianne out of the crawlspace. I kissed her repeatedly as she slapped me on the chest for not letting her help. I basically dragged her into the car and we got the hell out of Dodge.

We weren't able to salvage any of our cameras. We lost over $250,000 in equipment. But *we made it out alive.* After that, Dianne and I decided we finally wanted a baby. We tried dozens of times to write a response to the stories about the Rake on our website. To this day, the cryptid article on the website is the only one listed as "Status: Probable."

DEVIL'S DELINQUENTS

Okay, I'm not really good at text posts. Anyone who follows my Tumblr blog knows for sure that all I do is post fashion, food and felines. I'm in over my head with this one, but hopefully my small army of followers might be able to give me some insight as to what the hell is going on here.

It started about three weeks ago. You know the blog, KellyR8? Almost every one of my followers were also her followers as well. She ran that Louis Vuitton fashion blog. I reblogged her photos at least once or twice a day. She was the one with the really amazing custom Louis Vuitton theme and her profile photo appeared to be her. She had glassy blue eyes and platinum blonde hair.

She made a really long text post one afternoon. I never read text posts, but the title was "READ THIS PLEASE PLEASE I NEED HELP"

At the time, I didn't really think to save the text post. It was talking about this game called the Devil's Delinquents. Basically, it's a chain mail game. If someone nominates you (by sending you a death threat accompanied with directions on how to play), you have to write a disturbing, anonymous message to six different people about how you think they're going to die. By sending your threats to six people, you pick six people to send their messages next.

It sounds childish, but there's more to it than that. For example, in KellyR8's post, it said that the night after she played the game, she was up at three in the morning playing indie games on her computer. At first, she begins to hear whispering. As she took her headset off and listened, she realized that the house was silent, except for the whispers that sounded like they were coming from right next to her ear. Panicked, she turned on the lights, but it didn't help her much. She could clearly hear a man's deep voice reciting the message she sent to those people.

She made one final post later that day, but it sounded like she was losing her mind. She wrote that whatever you send as chain mail is how *YOU* will be killed. In her case, she wrote that the victims of the chain letter would die by having all of their nerves severed.

Last week, I went to write something in KellyR8's ask box just to see if she was okay, but her Tumblr had been deleted. Today, in my ask box, I got a chain letter under the title Devil's Delinquents. If I comply, I will be killed. If I don't send out any chain letters, will I still have to die? All I can remember is KellyR8 saying she had to send out the threats because if she didn't, the death threat she had received upon initiation into this fucked up game would be her manner of death.

Please, help me.

GREY

For as long as I can remember, my little sister has been locked away in McLean. That's the mental hospital in Massachusetts, and probably one of the best in the country, if not the absolute best. I was only eight years old when the incident occurred. For the most part, my parents kept me in the dark about what really happened to my sister. I only just found out her side of the story last night and I'm not exactly sure what to believe anymore.

The repetitive montage my parents always gave me throughout my entire life is a lie. That is, if I choose to believe a word from the girl who has become nothing but a stranger in a padded room. I know it's naïve, but something about her words and the way they flowed together made it very difficult for me to doubt her story. Sure, the doctors have thrown the label of hebephrenia, which has been explained to me as being disorganized schizophrenia. It just left me bewildered, seeing how my parents and the doctors viewed her in comparison to how I viewed her. They tossed her aside, cast her out of society and destroyed any hope of normalcy she could have ever had. She was a brilliant painter at the age of six, the time of the incident. I always believed that if they ever let her out, she would be the next Picasso. But keep in mind, before last night, it had been ten very long and confusing years without my sister.

At first, my parents would leave me with my grandparents and travel the three hours to see her every weekend. It was always a struggle for them to leave, as I would scream, cry, hit and bite in my failed attempts to force them to let me see her. Sure, older brothers have this reputation of being bullies to younger sisters, but that was never the case with Britney and me. I loved her more than anyone else in this world, my grandparents included. The year before, we were given the opportunity to give Britney her own bedroom to get her out of mine.

My parents had these weird ideas about gender roles and didn't believe a "growing young lady" should share a room with her older brother. Britney and I screamed and cried. I threw a lamp at my father. After a whole weekend of fighting, our parents relented and allowed us to continue sharing the room together. Let me be clear, there was nothing fucked up going on or anything like that. We were innocent children and I took the role of "big brother" extremely seriously. I argued that when they first brought my sister home from the hospital as a newborn, my father told me it was my job to help protect her. I made that my mission throughout my entire childhood and I felt like I would be betraying her if I let them move her bedroom away from mine. Britney had a terrible fear of closets and windows at night, and about three or four nights a week, she would come sleep in my bed on the bottom bunk, which was a full size in comparison to her twin bed above me. Britney would insist that a "big grey man" would watch her through our bedroom window. Though I always welcomed her into my bed, I never let her know my secret. For almost a year, I believed it was all in her head. One night, she crawled into my bed and cried into my shoulder, waking me up.

"Don't look," she whispered. "The big grey man is watching."

I never wanted to upset her, let alone the fact that I never believed her, so until that night, I never checked the window. I blinked the sleep away from my eyes and subtly glanced out the window. It wasn't intentional. I had no motivation to actually look. My eyes just happened to follow a brief movement on the other side of the glass. From the corner of my eye, I saw *something*. Whatever it was, it had a massive head and grey, sagging skin that covered protruding bones. For some reason, I didn't believe what I was seeing. I grabbed Britney and rolled her onto her side, facing me and keeping her back to the window. For about ten minutes, I was locked in a staring contest with whatever the fuck this thing was. The only movements it made was tilting its bulbous head from left to right quizzically. It seemed curious rather than menacing. Eventually, I blinked and the creature was gone. I believed I was having some kind of night terror and never spoke about this to anyone. I firmly believed Britney's story had gotten under my skin. Until last night, I rarely thought about the grey man at the window. It seemed almost like the remnants of a forgotten nightmare. It just didn't seem plausible to me.

As the weeks turned into months, my parents stopped going on their trips to visit Britney altogether. My parents actually *removed* all of the pictures of Britney from the photo frames around the house and even from the family photo album. When I discovered a missing school picture in the hallway, I went on a mad dash through the house, desperately trying to find a photo of my sister. My parents refused to acknowledge what they had done and sent me to my grandparents for a month. No matter how much I screamed and sobbed, there was no bringing the photos of my sister back. At school, I told the counselor that all the pictures were gone. She sat me down and told me that when something bad happens like this, it might be easier on my mom and dad to hide the pictures away for the time being. It took her three hours to convince me that it would be alright. I just couldn't stop crying. I wanted so desperately to see a photo of my sister. The counselor left me alone in the room for about twenty minutes. When she came back, she smiled, holding a book in her hand.

"This is the school yearbook that's coming out at the end of the year," she said, opening the book and looking at the kindergarten class my sister was in. She took a pair of scissors from her desk and cut out a photo of my sister. She handed it to me. "Keep it a secret. If your parents don't know, they can't take it away."

I had a velcro wallet at the time for my lunch money, and it had a couple of slots for pictures. It was the first picture I ever put in my first wallet. Over the years, I transferred that photo from wallet to wallet. I kept it in pristine condition as it was my prized possession.

When I got my license, my parents put a GPS tracking device in my first car. They wouldn't let me leave the city. When I turned eighteen last week, to put it briefly, I told them they could go fuck themselves, grabbed my shit and hit the road. I called my grandparents, who told me which hospital my sister was in. She was in *Massachusetts*. She really was only three hours away from my home in New Hampshire. I sped about half way there, but then slowed down to a speed so slow, it wasn't safe on the highway. What would I even say to a girl who's been locked up for ten years? Did she remember me? Did she even want to see me? Did Britney hate me for not being able to help her?

I showed my identification when I got in and they made me remove my belt and everything in my pockets. They led me down a long hallway and to a room on the right. They left me outside the door and told me to just knock and go in. The two nurses left me there and I stood outside the door for five minutes, unsure of what to say to my long lost best friend. Without overthinking it, I knocked on the door gently. I heard a frail, unfamiliar voice call from inside the room.

"Come in," she said. I realized Britney's voice had lost its high pitch over the years. Her words sounded almost monotone.

I entered the room to see my sister staring blankly at the door. A puzzled expression crossed her face. She wore loose hospital clothes and I gasped when I saw the scars of what had once been very deep cuts on her wrists. She didn't like my reaction and seemed very self-conscious, pulling the sleeves on her long shirt over her hands defensively.

"Who are you?" she asked. "What do you want?"

"It's me, Brit," I said, tears filling my eyes. "It's Brandon."

Britney stared at me for a long moment, but she stood up off her chair and came to face me. Her expression didn't change in the slightest. It was the most blank expression I had ever seen a human being wear. She approached me and lifted her left hand, touching the side of my face. I knew she always did this as a child when she would see a long lost relative.

"Brandon," she said flatly. "You left me here."

I instinctually wrapped her in an uncomfortably tight hug and sobbed loudly. "Brit, never. They hid you from me and I found you. I love you, Brit. Please. Please tell me why they did this to you. I want to help. I want to get you out of here and take you to live with me."

She hugged me gently and led me half-heartedly to a set of chairs. I sat down with her and she stared at the wall. She began speaking rapidly, but in a monotone voice.

"The incident," she said. "The Barbie clock said 11:08. It was the big grey man who opened the window, Brandon. You were still awake downstairs and watching a movie with dad. It happened so quickly. Everything went white, the man was the last thing I saw. Next thing I know I'm surrounded by white lights and several big, grey men. They touched me in bad places, tortured me, and said big words I didn't know. In the blink of an eye, I was back in bed facing the clock. It was 11:17. That's when I screamed. I kept screaming for days. They brought me to the hospital, then another and another. I've been here for years and no one believes me."

My mouth had fallen open in shock. All I remembered from that night was the screaming and my parents not letting me near my sister. The last time I saw her was when the ambulance brought her away. My memory flooded with images of the night I saw the big grey man outside the window. If she was crazy, why did I remember it? That's when I took action. I stood up and knelt in front of her, grabbing both sides of your face.

"Granddad gave me the number for this lawyer," I told her. "I'm not leaving until I can take you home. I'm getting an apartment, anywhere you want. It'll be like the old times. The times before this, all of this. Please, Brit, give me a chance. I just know I can get you out of here."

Britney did something that proved all of her doctors wrong. She *smiled*. Her type of schizophrenia was supposed to mean that she had something called the "flat effect," meaning she *doesn't* smile. If they were so right about her, why the fuck was she *smiling*?

"I love you, Brandon," she giggled, her voice regaining some of the childhood glee I remembered. "You're always there to save me."

I refused to leave the hospital last night. I'm typing this on my laptop using the hospital's Wi-Fi. No, I don't believe the doctors and I don't believe my parents or anyone else. I believe Britney and as I type this, two attorneys from the firm are filling out papers. The head doctor has agreed to release her into my custody, as she is only sixteen. This has eaten my entire savings from my high school job at Walmart. But I'll never tell Britney that I've barely got enough to get us a cheap place. I can get a job, but there's no way I'll be going to college. I'm hoping there's still hope for Britney. I'm determined to give her the normal life she was robbed of so many years ago. Six thousand dollars to get custody of my sister. My otal savings was just under fifteen thousand dollars. We'll be alright. We'll get by. I'll get a job and she can go to school, like she should be doing. They've got her tutors here and she's almost up to date on her education. I congratulated her for being on the road to graduating when she turns nineteen. I made a big deal and promised to take her on a shopping spree when we get out of here. I'm gonna make reservations at the nicest restaurant I can find. I'm gonna do all the shit my parents failed to do.

I'm looking at listings now. There's a one bedroom apartment in Maine that I can afford. All I need now is our old bunk bed from storage and a professional to install bars on all the windows. Whoever or whatever did this to her, to *us*, won't be coming back, even though Britney is sure that if she gets out, they will return for her. I've got a handgun on me at all times. My sister *will* live a normal life, but she will always carry the burden of the Greys on her shoulders.

GRANDDADDY

I guess you can say I was stupid, or perhaps even naïve. I'm a twenty-two-year-old woman. I live in the most remote region of Montana. I'm a city girl at heart, but the only life I've known is deep in the country. My parents died when I was young in a car accident that was too far away from civilization for any emergency personnel to arrive in time to save them. At first, they were missing. Days later, they were found dead. It doesn't affect me much. I was only two at the time and staying with my granddaddy. He worked as a mechanic at a local shop. He never got a lot of business, but all the locals went to him for their every vehicular need. Granddaddy taught me the value of hard work, elbow grease and how to take care of a car before I was even old enough to drive one.

I was driving down United States Highway 2. For those of you unfamiliar with my surroundings, it's notorious in all those big-city magazines as the "most dangerous highway" in America. I guess I never thought much about that, seeing as I'd been driving up and down that long stretch of road since I got my license. For many years, I'd driven through the great state of Montana on that deserted path. Sure, it's a highway alright, but if you're there for too long or if you go too ar, slowly but surely all your fellow drivers seem to vanish. The further from home you get, the less people you come across.

I'm a country girl, even though Granddaddy always told me I'd grow up to be a city girl like my mama. Mama was a movie star. Well, that's what Granddaddy always tells me. Really, she lived for a few years up in California. Granddaddy always makes those years of my mama's life sound so glamorous, but Aunt Suzanne got drunk at a family barbecue and said mama was a street-walker, hoping to find some fat cat to give her a big break up in the Berkeley Hills. Granddaddy slapped his daughter, my Aunt Suzanne, right across her face. In all my years, I've never seen my granddaddy get angry. Hell, from the looks of all my kin, I'd wager no one at the oak picnic table *ever* saw Granddaddy angry. From that moment all along through the rest of the night, not one person had the audacity to say a damned word. It was the quietest barbecue in all my life. Only time I'd ever heard anything so quiet was on a hunting trip with Granddaddy when I was a kid. Those deep, dark woods got real quiet right before we saw a coyote strut right on pass our newly pitched tent. Granddaddy warned me that when nature gets quiet, shit's about to go wild and you'd better keep your trap shut if you don't want to end up dead as a doornail. That's what happened at that barbecue, and I'd swear on a stack of Holy Bibles that nobody in my family ever crossed Granddaddy again. Nobody spoke about my mother ever again, and if they did, the words were kind. Never speak ill of the dead in front of a holy man like Granddaddy.

Granddaddy is a soft-spoken, plump old-timer who always has a can of Pabst Blue Ribbon in his hand and a fat lump of chewing tobacco in his mouth. Once he got home from the shop, he'd spend all the twilight hours on his rocker out on the wrap-around porch. He'd drink a six pack and spit his tobacco in that old, grey bucket that I don't believe he ever emptied in my whole life. It smelled sometimes, but that scent was the smell of home.

Every Sunday, Granddaddy would wake up at the crack of dawn to drive his red pickup out to the pond a couple of miles away. He'd bring bird seed and feed all the ducks while reading his Sunday paper. He'd make it back home by seven in the morning, and I learned young I'd damned well be dressed and ready for Sunday service when he got home. If I slept late, Granddaddy wouldn't wait for me. He'd drive his pickup into town and leave my ass to walk four miles in my Sunday dress. I never tested what he would do if I didn't make it to church. Granddaddy was a man nobody ever wants to cross.

So, Granddaddy is why I was out in the middle of nowhere up on Highway 2 late that night. I had been away from home, doing my studies in agriculture. Every month, I'd travel up that long, barren road and visit Granddaddy for the weekend. The drive took hours and I always got to the house at around half past three in the morning. No matter what time I'd make it home, Granddaddy would be rocking in his chair on the porch. I had a feeling he'd stay up all night, making sure I got in safely. He'd always have a mug of black coffee and a warm smile. He'd always take my luggage from me and when I told him I could manage, Granddaddy said a real man always gets the bags for the lady. All my life, Granddaddy respected women and he taught me that I deserved good, fair treatment. Chivalry ain't dead; you all just aren't looking at gentlemen like my Granddaddy. I'd pour myself a cup of his freshly brewed local store brand coffee, sit out on the porch with him and watch the sunrise.

That night, I was really looking forward to that cup of caffeinated goodness. My eyes were heavy and I knew I only had about an hour and a half left to go. I felt like if I could just close my eyes for a couple of minutes, I'd make it to the house by four in the morning. I knew there was a little rest stop coming up in a few miles. Well, let me be clear, it was a Highway 2 rest stop and it wasn't close to much of anything at all. No bathrooms, no food and nothing but a six-car parking lot. Never had I heard about anybody stopping at those lots, let alone in the middle of the night.

I'm gonna stress this again. I'm a wannabe city girl, but in my heart and soul, I was raised country. Stranger-danger didn't exist in my world because our tiny town was an everybody-knows-everybody kind of place. Either way, I hadn't seen another car in hours and I figured it couldn't hurt anything to stop for twenty minutes.

I pulled into the lot and turned off the engine on my old, beat up minivan. I checked the locks on the doors and chuckled to myself. There wasn't a living soul out in these parts for miles. I'd be fine to rest. I closed my eyes and think I might have begun to have a dream about this boy Roger Connally, the cute boy who worked one of the two registers at the local mart.

Suddenly, a loud crash shook me from my slumber and I screamed loudly. Glass covered me from my head to my old canvas sneakers. My window had been busted in, but oh, I had bigger problems than that. A big, strong hand was grabbing my throat, digging ragged fingernails into my skin. I gasped for air and flailed around for dear life. It was a big man wearing a flannel button-up and a baseball cap. I couldn't see his face and I didn't want to see his face.

My memory flashed back to the thoughts I had been consumed with while still on the road. I remembered Granddaddy slapping Aunt Suzanne right upside her crooked lipstick. He didn't say a word to her. He came to my side and patted me on the shoulder.

"When you're in a pinch, little girl, you either man up or get out."

Sure, Granddaddy had been talking about defending his dead daughter and telling Aunt Suzanne to take a long hike off a short pier. But something in my brain clicked and I realized I couldn't man up, so I had to get the hell out of there. I reached for the keys and started the engine. Before the man could stop me, I threw that shift into drive and sped off, my head slamming back up against the ripped, leather headrest as the force of the man's grip was yanked from my neck. With a busted window this time of year, the ride home wouldn't be pleasant, but that was the least of my worries. I checked the rearview mirrors and realized the man was fading into the distance. He'd hopped into a shitbox sedan and took off going the opposite direction. Through my tears, I giggled softly to myself, remembering what Granddaddy said after he gave me a good talking-to for not speaking up when I saw Linda Beller steal a pack of Hubba Bubba from the local mart. I had waited until we got back into the car to tell Granddaddy what I'd seen. He turned the car off and looked me in the eye, like he always did when I was in trouble.

"Bad people do bad things, but if you let them get away with it, not only are you bad, but you're a coward. No grandbaby of mine is a coward. You go in there and pay with your allowance for what you just did. Tom owns this shop and he's a hard-working man. You kept your mouth shut, now you gotta pay up."

Bad people do bad things. The man who had attacked me was a *bad* person. But this time, instead of paying the price after the fact, Granddaddy's lesson taught me I had better not grow up to be a coward. As I cried, I realized how proud my Granddaddy would be. He always worried so much, and I could finally tell him I got myself out of trouble and I *wasn't* a coward, just like he taught me.

Pulling in to the long drive-way at around four in the morning, I saw Granddaddy sitting on his rocker. He wore a blue dress shirt and faded gray slacks that I recognized as his Sunday service clothes. I rushed out of the car, sobbing loudly as I ran up to him. For the first time in all my years, Granddaddy didn't wait up for me. If he was awake, he'd be off his ass and grabbing his rifle, seeing my window smashed in and all that. Not wanting to wake him up to bad news, I carried my luggage up to my room without Granddaddy. As I tossed the bag on the bed, I realized this wasn't right. Granddaddy *never* let me carry my luggage and he was *always* wide-eyed and bushy-tailed when I made my way home once a month. I ran out to the porch, screen-door slamming loudly behind me. Granddaddy didn't even stir. Fearing the worst, I reached out and touched his hand. He was cold as ice and dead as a doornail. His coffee was still warm, resting on the table beside him next to his chewing tobacco.

"Granddaddy," I said, salty tears in my eyes. I sighed and sat next to him, shaking my head. "Just like a man. Just like a fucking man."

I didn't call up the Sheriff just yet. I wanted to sit there for one last sunrise with my Granddaddy. I drank his coffee and for the first time in my young life, chewed his tobacco as the sun rose over the horizon.

TO GIVE UP SMOKING

My name is Cynthia. I started smoking Newport cigarettes when I was nine years old. I'm currently thirty-one. I'm recently divorced and unable to have children, but I had hoped to adopt a little one. Hell, even a teenager. I don't really care. I just wanted someone to keep me company to end the every-night routine of eating a pint of ice cream, smoking three packs of cigarettes and watching reruns of sitcoms from the '80s. Hell, if I didn't have work four days a week, I'd never leave my couch. I'm overweight, balding in my early thirties and looking for something more productive to do with my life.

I had been watching the Times Square New Year's Eve event alone in my shitty apartment. Some celebrity had been asking random people in the crowd about their New Year's resolutions. Some wanted a new car, some wanted a better job, some had their priorities fucked up. It was just the usual New Year's garbage I'd been dealing with my whole life. I had always meant to have a list of at least three resolutions, but either never thought of anything or never followed through.

It was strange, the commercial I saw. It had bright colors and a woman dancing with some cute guy in some sort of studio. The music was louder than the normal television volume and it immediately grabbed my attention, startling me because of the sudden noise. A woman's voice began speaking over the upbeat music.

"New year: new you! Tired of wasting your time, your money and your health on that nasty cigarette habit? Ask your doctor if Fumafeur is right for you!"

Fumafeur? Was this some kind of new method to giving up smoking? I put out my cigarette in the ashtray on the end table and perked up a bit.

"Fumafeur is one simple pill a day for thirty days. It must be prescribed by your doctor. Fumafeur may help you lose weight, so ask your doctor if Fumafeur is right for you."

It's a win-win! Not only could I finally kick the cigarettes to the curb, but I could potentially lose weight? There *was* this new diet plan my coworker Ashley had been bragging about. Normally, I don't feed into that sort of hype, but I watched her lose so much weight in only a month that I had asked her for the brochure. I was sure it was still in my purse.

"Side effects may include abnormal sleep, loss of appetite, sore throat, headache, nausea, skin rash, mild constipation, or new or worsening mood changes. Contact your doctor immediately if you experience—"

I wasn't listening anymore. I put my ice cream down, opened my laptop and logged in to my doctor's patient portal. I loved this new portal thing because I could log in, check when he's available and see when appointments have been canceled. It's much easier to get an appointment and I can even let him know what the appointment is for. A few years ago, it took weeks to get an appointment. This system made sure I could easily get in whenever I needed to.

I had decided on my three resolutions. I got an appointment with my doctor to discuss weight loss, quitting smoking and possibly getting my hair to grow back. In a few minutes, one of the 24-hour answering service people confirmed my appointment for January 2nd at 9AM and let me know that my physician always recommends this over the counter cream unless I have a skin condition. She also wrote that if I am wary of it, wait to ask the doctor. I looked up the stuff and saw amazing results, so I ordered a six-month supply and had it delivered on the same day as my appointment. I decided that once that ball dropped, I wasn't going to bed. I was going to actually *clean* my apartment. I had just gotten one of those new, fancy coffee makers with those little pods. I made myself a cup and sipped it as the new year was celebrated in New York City.

I spent the entirety of New Year's Day cleaning my apartment from top to bottom. New year, new me, right? I basically had to go through everything I owned because I had become quite the pack-rat, leaving me with limited space.

After filling fourteen large, black garbage bags with things I didn't want to bring into the new year with me, I carried them three or four at a time to the dumpster in the back of my apartment building. Coffee after coffee and the entire place was spotless. I even finally got around to unpacking two boxes from when I had moved in *years* ago. I remembered I used to wear significantly smaller clothes, and instead of throwing them all away, I organized my closet. The fat clothes on the left, the new-year-new-me clothes on the right.

It was five in the evening and I was exhausted. Satisfied with my new, clean apartment, I went to bed early, knowing I would need to be well-rested for my appointment the following morning. The doctor seemed to be in a rush. He told me the brand of hair cream I was using was great and gave me two new prescriptions. The first was an appetite suppressant and the second was my new, exciting wonder-drug. I went to the pharmacy and got them both filled immediately. Then I went to the grocery store and actually bought *healthy food* to cook and not something I would throw in the microwave for two and a half minutes.

I made myself a nice dinner for the first time since I was in my early twenties. I took both the pills and felt fine. All those side effect warnings were bull shit, as usual. I decided a reasonable, new bed time would be ten. I tucked myself in and found it difficult to fall asleep. I thought about maybe getting a feline companion to keep me company. I dropped the idea when I realized I'm compulsive and would immediately become the crazy cat lady.

Eventually, I think I fell asleep, but it wasn't like anything I remember. I think it was a dream, but I can't be sure. I was lying on my back, seeing the room around me shrouded in the darkness of the night. I thought I was awake and struggled, trying to move. My limbs felt too heavy to even twitch and I got very nervous. I could have sworn I saw moving shadows out of the corner of my eye. I'm not sure when it happened, but I jolted awake, soaked with sweat and gasping loudly.

It was just a dream, I thought, trying to calm myself down. I remembered reading some article online about sleep paralysis. I wondered if that was what I had experienced. I checked the clock to see it was about twenty minutes before m alarm went off. I got dressed up in my favorite red blouse with the buttons and pu on a *skirt* for the first time in as long as I could remember. I was surprised it fit. I even went as far as to put on a pair of uncomfortable heels, but I would just be at my desk. I spent extra time on my hair and makeup, feeling proud of how I looked. New year, new me.

Everyone at the office complimented my appearance. Cindy from accounting said I looked like a "brand new woman." I was beaming with pride ar on my lunch break, I went outside to smoke, but decided against it. I threw my pack of cigarettes away and went to the little deli across the street to get myself a salad. I went to the break room instead of eating at my desk and got many kind words and compliments. I bragged about my new attitude and lifestyle choices and received nothing but support.

Fast forward a week and a half. I lost twelve pounds, dropped a dress size and noticed my legs appearing thinner. I was ecstatic. It didn't come without hard work and it didn't come without side effects. I found myself vomiting every morning and it had become a ritual. I would only eat two small meals a day and a smoothie I would make after work. I didn't notice the hair growth cream working and I knew it was supposed to take a month, but I didn't want to wait. Everything else about me looked better. I went and got my nails done and they looked just as fancy as the younger girls in the office. I had saved a large sum of money for a new car, but decided the car could wait. I basically paid three thousand dollars to get hair *put in* and then have some kind of electricity thing scheduled once a week for three weeks. I was assured that if my hair was not growing normally within those three weeks, I would receive a full refund. I had only been to one grueling, painful session, but my head definitely felt different. The fake hair looked so real. I was told it would fall out when real hair grew in to replace it.

So it sounds like everything was going great, right? There were problems. Every night, I could only sleep a few hours. The night terrors and sleep paralysis progressively got worse, leading me to upgrade from coffee to espresso and to buy Adderall from a coworker. I'm not gonna lie, I was hyper all the time and full of energy. But my body ached and I knew I needed more sleep. I brushed it off, and decided that if it got worse, I would go back to the doctor.

It was day thirteen of the Fumafeur that something very strange happened. was in a meeting with my coworkers giving a presentation. Everyone in the room loved the advertising idea and I was praised. I'm always a very bubbly person, always smiling to the point that it takes twenty minutes to cover my laugh lines with makeup in the morning. Then Cindy spoke up.

"I like the presentation," she said. "Fiscally, however, this isn't going to work."

Normally, I would have smiled and asked her to explain and let me know what we could change. Disagreements happen all the time, but I'm not one to eve really get emotional. I always chuckle, apologize if I've wronged someone and generally be kind to others just like my mother taught me. No one was ever mean to me and if they were, I would reply so kindly that they would always be nicer after. My smile drooped into a frown I didn't know I was capable of.

"What do you mean?" I said, suddenly feeling like I was holding back tears.

"It's a minor adjustment," she clarified. "We may want to start with only five or six thousand brochures, test the waters and—"

"No!" I gasped, feeling a tear slide down my cheek. My behavior was not my own and I was not in control. I literally stomped my feet twice like a child throwing a temper tantrum. "No, no, no! Stop it."

Ashley and Cindy exchanged confused expressions, then Ashley got up and approached me nervously.

"Cynthia, are you alright?" she gasped. "You're not yourself. What's going on?"

"Nobody ever appreciates me!" I said, raising my voice and shaking my head repeatedly. I compulsively began to slap myself repeatedly in the face. Everyone in the room gasped and Ashley made a move to grab my wrists.

"Oh, my gosh," she said, wrapping me in a hug. "Honey, no, no, we love you. It isn't about you. You're great, perfect even. Please, I think you're having some kind of problem and we should get you checked out. This isn't okay. I'm worried. We're all worried."

I suddenly felt humiliated. I covered my face and sobbed loudly, running out of the room and tripping over my high heels. I fell to the floor and curled into a ball, admitting defeat and screaming loudly. Before I knew it, I was rushed into an ambulance and brought to the local hospital. After evaluation and being given a sedative, I felt like my old self again. I felt humiliated and ridiculous for what had happened, but Ashley stood by my side and insisted I didn't do anything wrong and nobody was judging me. The doctors said I had a nervous breakdown, probably due to all the major life changes I was dealing with. Ashley held my hand and smiled at me.

"See? You're alright and I'm so proud of you," Ashley said reassuringly.

The doctors sent me home with a month's worth of sedatives to take when I get "nervous." I was told to get refills from my doctor. They weighed me, once I calmed down, and I couldn't believe it. That day alone, I was down three pounds. Ashley decided to drive me home that night, promising to pick me up for work the next morning so I could just take my car home the next day. She stayed with me, we cooked dinner together and I told her about my two sides of my closet. She insisted that my clothes were starting to look way too big on me and basically rushed me into the bedroom to try on my small clothes. I fit into about half of the outfits and we decided to pop open a bottle of this wine I'd gotten for Christmas. I hesitated because I remember the package on the Fumafeur saying something about not drinking, but Ashley promised it would be fine.

"You're home," she said with a laugh, pouring two completely filled wine glasses and handing me one. "Hell, if you lend me that blue dress, I'll stay the night to keep an eye on you. No need to pick you up tomorrow morning. We'll just go in together."

"You'd really want to?" I asked. No one ever wanted to keep me company.

"Uh, duh?" Ashley said. "Cynthia, you're really a great friend. I hope we can be best friends. You're like the big sister I never got to have."

Ashley and I had a wild night together. We stayed up way too late and eventually passed out in the living room with Madonna songs playing on repeat. This was when the night terrors changed dramatically. I wasn't just seeing shadows anymore. They weren't shadows at all. The large window behind the sofa I slept on had black, shadow hands reaching out and trying to grab me. The heating system went on automatically with a soft rumble. I was frozen and paralyzed in a dream-like state, once again unable to move my limbs. I became paranoid, or at least I think I was being paranoid. I thought the heating system was talking about hurting me and when the icemaker in the freezer made that annoying sound it always makes, in my mind, it was the refrigerator talking to the heating system about raping me and Ashley.

I woke up screaming. I startled Ashley awake and she began forcing me to swallow sedatives while I screamed and cried about the appliances trying to rape us. After about an hour, I calmed down and felt fine again. This had really scared the shit out of Ashley, though. Ashley gave me a phone number for her psychiatrist. She confided in me that she took antidepressants and said I needed to call her. Ashley and I both took the day off work and she drove me to the appointment. It was considered "urgent" enough to get me right in. Ashley waited in the car and took a nap, I think.

I talked to the psychiatrist and told her about the sedatives. I felt like I was hiding the fact that I was taking diet supplements and Fumafeur. I don't know why, but I felt ashamed of who I had once been and I was about halfway through my month-long plan. A couple of incidents were no reason to spoil it. Plus, I couldn't open the can of worms of me buying Adderall. She seemed to think it was stress, prescribed me a stronger sedative and even gave me a sleep medication. She warned me that it could be very addictive and that she would only write it for month to "regulate" my sleep schedule.

Ashley took me to my car, we hugged and agreed to do brunch the next day. I filled my new prescriptions and realized I spent an awful lot of time in pharmacies these days. I had a lot of time to kill, so I walked down Main Street nd looked at all the stores. I wasn't saving for a car anymore and I thought treating myself would help brighten up the bad week I was having.

I bought a lot of new clothes and for some reason, when I tried some of them on, they were too big. I wasn't sure how, but the size I had tried on the night before was too loose and the woman suggested a size two. I hadn't been a size two since college! I bounced up and down happily and brought a dozen bags to my car, ignoring the fact that I had just blown over five hundred dollars. I decided new year, new me. I even went to this place down the street Cindy had gotten her adjustments made. I had wrinkles and with my hair sorted out, I wondered if I could get injections like her. Her face looked so great. They tried to warn me that insurance didn't cover it, it was quite expensive and there were a lot of risks, blah blah blah. I realized if I played my cards right, I could get this done. I paid more than I bargained for and was told to go home and not take the little bandages off for two hours. I was told to lie down and put a cold bag of peas on my face for the two hours. I rushed home, didn't bother to put my new clothes away and listened to music while I waited. The concept of time just didn't make sense to me anymore. What felt like one minute had actually been an hour and a half. I just didn't understand time anymore and I wondered what the drugs could possibly be doing to my brain. I was so close to being the perfect woman and I even heard that one of the corporate attorneys was planning to ask me to dinner. My face felt numb and apparently, it would stay that way for as long as two weeks. I looked in the mirror and was happy enough with the results. New year, new me. Less time putting on makeup in the morning because those lines were gone, baby!

I decided to stop the appetite suppressant that night. I figured if I kept eating healthy, I could maintain my new weight. I did, however, take the new sleeping medication and the Fumafeur. It was alright at first. I had dreams that were strange, but no paralysis. I woke up in the middle of the night, groggy and confused. I think I went to the kitchen and got seltzer water. Next thing I know, I'm back in bed, frozen in my body. This time, things were *so* much worse. I heard voices telling me to do horrible things, telling me that everyone hated me and the hands were *touching* me and I could feel them grabbing and pulling my skin off my bones. I shot awake ten minutes before my alarm and gripped my head. I felt hungover and confused. I immediately took a shit ton of Adderall and drank espresso to try and break me out of this fog I was in. By the time I finished my shower, I was back to normal...well, sort of.

The voices were still there, even though I wasn't dreaming. I heard an occasional whisper that sounded like my name and I was beginning to think the curling iron was the one doing the talking. I thought about it as I applied makeup to my aching face gently and realized it didn't make sense. The curling iron had to take orders from someone, and I knew it was the refrigerator.

Every now and again during my morning routine, I would argue with the voices. Eventually, I realized I could hear them, but they couldn't hear me. That's because they were using remote controlled alien technology from another universe to control the appliances and get them to speak English to me, but the appliances themselves couldn't understand anything I said. It was a one-sided conversation, basically. Even if the aliens heard me through the microphones they put in my apartment, they wouldn't answer. Otherwise the CIA would come and I would know too much. The people on that morning news show could hear the voices too and I chuckled every time one of them stopped talking to listen to the voices. It was like they would forget what they were going to say because they were being interrupted. I realized I was given a gift and they were only threatening to rape me and make me kill all the microbes to gain control over me. I wouldn't give them the satisfaction and eventually I learned to tune out the voices.

I arrived at work right on time and realized that they had bugged the office too. The surround sound was playing jazz music and whispering I couldn't understand and the lights seemed to be too bright. I realized not everyone in the office was smart enough to know what was going on, so I kept my information to myself. I didn't want the CIA to come and get me.

Work was a blur. Countless pills were taken every time the voices got to be too much to handle. I even started seeing the shadows and the hands. But the pills made it easier because they kept a smile on my face. No one noticed that I knew the secrets.

I got home late and took my Fumafeur and my sleeping medication. While I waited for the sleep medication to work, I checked my E-mail and turned on some music to drown out the voices. I had over a dozen E-mails from my doctor's office, telling me to call them immediately because there's been an emergency. I picked up my cell phone, which was still on silent from the day at work and I had three missed calls. I couldn't focus on the doctor's words in the voicemails, but I recognized it was his voice and not a secretary. He said something about psychiatric medical records coming in and something about the Fumafeur. I couldn't understand his garbled speech, so I figured he was reminding me to take it and saying it was good that I went to see a psychiatrist. That had to be the point. Maybe he was praising me. I couldn't focus on the phone over the sound of the voices and I had to hurry to type out an E-mail to his office thanking them for the Fumafeur and letting them know I haven't smoked a single cigarette since I began my treatment. I knew I had to follow through the entire thirty days though, just like the box said. I didn't want to risk getting back into that nasty habit.

I had to stop typing mid-sentence and send the E-mail as it was. It was getting difficult to read what I wrote and I realized that the message didn't say anything I wanted it to. It was so riddled with typos and weird phrases that I didn emember what I had meant to type. I figured they would understand it because they're doctors and all that, so I sent it as it was.

Within minutes, I fell asleep right there on the couch. I was once again frozen and all the voices were telling me a message. I tried my best to make it out and twitch my fingers, but everything was so confusing. The shadows were no longer just hands and vague figures. I saw shadow men I recognized as the alien leadership in charge. They were telling me the CIA was planning to take me to a place far away so I couldn't tell the world about the real alien government. I began hearing a banging sound coming from the kitchen. It sounded like knocking and I vaguely heard two men screaming for me to open the door. I realized it was the CIA and tried desperately to wake up, but I couldn't budge an inch no matter how hard I tried. I heard a crash and then I remember hearing voices, but they sounded human. The shadows promised to hide me and blackness consumed me.

I woke up this morning in a hospital bed with my arms strapped down and a needle in my arm. I realized I was being held hostage by the CIA. The voices were making me bite my tongue until it bled and a loud beeping sound came from the right side of the room. A few people in hospital scrubs ran into the room and began checking my mouth. It was bleeding a lot and they put some kind of alien device in my mouth like a gag so I couldn't close my teeth. I tried to talk to them, but I slurred in a way I had never heard myself speak before and the hard, plastic piece was stopping me from closing my mouth. A man in a white coat rushed to my side and began yelling at the nurses.

"Give me morphine, quickly, quickly," he said, securing gloves on his hand and applying some kind of gauze to the inside of my mouth. Everything just felt wet, and then everything felt numb. I could still hear the voices and see the shadows, but it was as if none of it made any sense to me. They were trying to stop me from communicating.

My eyes darted around the room very quickly. My body was once again impossible to move, but I was *awake* and I *knew it*. I saw a nurse accept somethin from the doctor with his hands in my mouth and I think they thought I was asleep. I saw what appeared to be my *tongue* being put into one of those little plastic cups they use for urine samples. Once the doctor finished whatever he was doing, my eyes were closed, but I could hear him more clearly over the jumble of voices.

"Psychosis, clear case," he said to someone in the room. "Possibly much worse, but we'll need to see the MRI results. I need you to contact her next of kin and let them know she is being committed legally and if they want to fight it in court, so be it."

None of the words seemed to make any sense to me. Everything was so clear and yet, it sounded like I was under water. I heard his voice echo and then I heard a very familiar voice. I think it might have been my doctor's voice, but I can't be sure.

"Shit, shit," I heard him say. I'd never heard him swear before. "I couldn't get in contact with Cynthia to let her know about the Fumafeur recall. She sent this bizarre E-mail to my staff and I called her an ambulance. They kicked in her door and thank God they did."

He sounded quite upset. The doctor who had taken my tongue away let out strange, almost chuckle. "These things happen to the best of us. Permanent brain damage is likely, but we won't know for sure until the results come through."

"I feel terrible about this," my doctor said. "I had no idea—"

"No one did," the man interrupted. "Not our problem. Let the pharmaceutical company get the shit sued out of them by this girl's family. I think her parents are coming from upstate to voluntarily give us the go ahead, so we'll have some time on the whole legal bull shit."

"Her mother is my friend," the man sighed. "Jesus. What the fuck am I gonna tell her?"

The strange man laughed quietly. "I don't get paid enough to give you life advice."

A female laughed and sounded like she was talking to the strange doctor. It sounded like they were leaving because even though they sounded far away before they sounded even further in the distance and in moments, I couldn't hear them at all. I just heard some weird gargling noise that left me feeling anxious and a bit confused.

"I don't know if you can hear me," my doctor said. "Cynthia, I'm so sorry. Christ, of course you can't hear me. Get a hold of yourself, Jack. Right, okay. I'm talking to a vegetable. I need a drink."

BEHIND THE SHOWER CURTAIN

Even as a young girl, as far back as my memory goes, I have *always* checked behind the shower curtain any time I entered a bathroom. I don't understand it. I've never been afraid of the dark, monsters under my bed or even horror movies for that matter. I was never a frightened little girl. My whole family and all my friends actually called me things like "brave" and "fearless" my entire life. I suppose I still have that type of reputation, but alas, I *always* check behind the shower curtain when entering a bathroom.

I've done it since I could walk. It's one of my first memories. Every time I enter a bathroom, anxiety floods through my body and I freeze up for a moment. In a wild burst of adrenaline that never seems to fail me, I harshly fling aside the shower curtain and find an empty bath tub. I would always sigh with relief, chuckle quietly and go about whatever business I had in the bathroom. It wasn't even only when I was going to shower or use the toilet. It was *every single time* I entered the bathroom, without fail. If I had to get something from the medicine cabinet, I had to check behind the shower curtain. If I had to blow my nose, I had to check behind the shower curtain. It's something that is so deeply ingrained in me that I don't think I'll ever be able to enter a bathroom and *not* look behind the shower curtain...especially considering what I saw there when I was nine years old.

My father took off when my mom got pregnant with me. I've never met him and I don't have any plans on meeting him in the future. I'm in my mid-twenties now, and these memories would have faded at least somewhat, if I could ever allow myself to break free of my ritualistic shower surveillance. I still do it, and now, I know I always will. I still feel a wave of terror rush over me whenever I enter a bathroom and remember I have to check. I've tried *not* checking, but I always cave before a moment even passes. I always talk myself out of *not* checking.

What if there's a person? What if there's a monster? What if a raccoon is in there?

I think of every possible scenario, mostly ridiculous and impossible, but others somewhat probable while still being significantly unlikely. I imagine all kinds of things waiting for me behind the dreaded curtain. There's only ever been one time in my entire life that I flung that curtain aside to see something absolutely horrifying. I always wondered what I would do if something was actually in there. I suppose when it happened, I froze up for a second or two. Not that it made much of a difference in the end, but if it had been a serial killer or a monster, those precious seconds could have cost me my life.

I remember that day so vividly, and my therapist says I'll always remember it like it just happened yesterday. I walked up the stairs, arriving home from my long day at school. I began to go into the bathroom, but I stopped. I always put off using the bathroom because it was this entire ritual of checking behind the shower curtain. I put it off, stifling the urge to pee. I went back downstairs and grabbed a candy bar from the snack drawer. Eating it carefully, I turned on the television and remember Tom and Jerry being on for just a second. By the time I finished my three bites of chocolate, the show was on the credits and the three 'clock Bugs Bunny show was almost on. I decided that if I didn't want to miss it, I had to run upstairs to the bathroom. I darted up the stairs, realizing I only had a short commercial break to do my business. Arriving in the bathroom, I lifted my hand to the light switch, but dropped my hand to my side. The bathroom's window was letting in a bright, afternoon light and I didn't really need to turn on the light. It was so bright in the bathroom that it just wasn't necessary. Natural lighting always had a way of making me feel braver.

I hesitated before reaching for the shower curtain. Could today possibly be the day? I could just *not* look behind the shower curtain. I stared at it for a moment and giggled to myself nervously.

Not today, I thought silently. *I'm gonna be ten in a few weeks. I've got to learn how to be brave, even when no one's looking.*

For the first and only time in my life, I pulled down my pants and sat on the toilet. I couldn't get myself to pee because I kept thinking about what could possibly be behind the shower curtain. I knew if I could just get this over with, that would be a conquered fear and it would give me a sense of accomplishment. Finally, I let the stream of urine go and my thoughts drifted to my D+ in History on my report card. I dreaded showing my mother.

Mother. As I stood up and pulled my pants up around my waist, I began to think about my mom. Where was she? She was normally waiting downstairs for me when I got home. I began to think maybe she had plans to go out today and I just didn't remember her telling me. It was strange, but it wouldn't be the first time something like that happened. Then again, *I* didn't worry about being home alone. It was the late 1980's and people in my neighborhood left their kids home alone all the time. Hell, we didn't even lock our doors. It just wasn't something we thought about at the time.

I washed my hands and as I turned off the water, I heard a sound coming from the bathtub. I whirled around and nearly jumped out of my skin. I realized I heard the quiet tap of water dripping into a pool of water. Maybe mother had left the bathtub dripping.

Then it hit me. It didn't sound like a drop or two of water hitting the *bottom of the empty bathtub.* It sounded familiar, like the tap dripping when I was sitting in a full bath. The color drained from my face and after a moment of deliberation, I remembered something. Mom was supposed to clean this morning. Maybe she left the bathtub soaking in bleach, like she sometimes did. The bleach wasn't burning my nose though, so that was ruled out. Maybe she left that bucket she used for mopping the floors filled underneath the dripping tap. I couldn't be sure and there was really only one way to find out.

Putting on my bravest face, I reached a quivering hand up to grab the floral shower curtain. In one quick movement, I flung the curtain open, stumbling backward against the sink like I sometimes did. It was like my brain couldn't process what I was seeing and everything just kind of froze up on me for a minute or two. The bathtub was *filled* with a deep, red liquid. I knew it was blood, but I was trying to rationalize some other explanation. Then I looked at the end of the tub and saw what appeared to be *hair*. I realized it was a head, bobbing up and down softly in the pool of blood. Then I looked a bit closer and let out a loud shriek. It wasn't just a head. It was my mother's head. It was my mother's head attached to her pale, lifeless corpse.

And so I screamed. I screamed and screamed until my throat became raspy and dry as the Sahara. When I finally got my legs to move, I began running down the hallway and down the stairs. I fell about halfway down, tripping over my own shoes. I landed at the bottom on my back and felt the wind get knocked right out of me. My front door swung open and Mrs. Belton from next door ran to my side.

"Beatrice? Beatrice, what's all the screaming?" She ran to my side and helped me up. "Are you alright? Did you get hurt? Where's your mother?"

I couldn't answer her. I raised a trembling finger and pointed up the stairs t the bathroom door. I then screamed and screamed some more, tears rushing down both sides of my face. Mrs. Belton ran up the stairs and I heard her gasp when she reached the bathroom door. She saw what I had seen and came running down the stairs, grabbing me by the arm and yanking me out of the house.

Before I knew it, fire trucks, three police cars and two ambulances were blocking off my street. All the neighborhood kids watched my mother's body get wheeled out on a gurney, but it was covered in a black bag. The paramedics at on of the ambulances were checking me out. I had a big bruise on my back from falling and I had hit the back of my head, which was bleeding a little bit. When a crisis worker showed up, she talked to me for a little while, but I couldn't answer her. I couldn't move or speak at all. She said something about inpatient care and

The ambulance took me to a building with a white hospital room. They hooked all these needles into my arm and had me lie down. They said they put something in the needle to make me sleep for a while, and the last thing I remember seeing was Mr. and Mrs. Belton with their twin boys rushing into the room. Everything went black after that.

After a few hours, I awoke and was sent home with the Belton family. They lived right next door to where I had lived, and after a few weeks, they had packed up everything to move me to their new house across town. Mrs. Belton promised they were planning to move anyway, but I heard Mr. and Mrs. Belton talking in the kitchen in hushed whispers about a mortgage they couldn't afford all to get me away from the neighborhood. They took me in and raised me like their own. We didn't talk about my mother's suicide until after I graduated from college. To this day, no one knows why she did it. She didn't leave a note, she didn't act differently. There were simply no clues as to what could have driven my mother to slit her wrists in the tub that afternoon. And I suppose I don't want to know why she did it. Sure, there's this nagging in the back of my mind every now and again that leaves me wondering if it was my fault. The Beltons always assure me that my mother was having a mid-life crisis and that it had nothing to do with me. I still find that all very hard to believe, but I get by just fine. I have a great life. I just have to go to therapy once a week and I *always* have to check behind the shower curtain. I'll probably be doing that for the rest of my natural life.

Made in the USA
Middletown, DE
27 December 2018